LION

0-60: 4.1 seconds
TOP SPEED: 90kmph
WEIGHT: 803kg
HEIGHT: 198cm
MEAN-NESS: 9.9/10
BRAINS: 2/10

VS

Rabbit

0-60: -
TOP SPEED: 45kmph
WEIGHT: 2kg
HEIGHT: 36cm
MEAN-NESS: 1/10
BRAINS: 9/10

by Alex Latimer

PICTURE CORGI

In memory of my mother, Margery

LION VS RABBIT A PICTURE BOOK

A CORGI BOOK 978 0 552 574 501

First published in Great Britain by Picture Corgi, an imprint of Random House Children's Books A Random House Group Company

This edition Published 2013

1 2 3 4 5 6 7 8 9 10

Copyright © Alex Latimer, 2013

The right of Alex Latimer to be identified as the author and illustrator of this work has been asserted in accordance with the Copyright, Designs and Patents Act 1988.

Picture Corgi Books are published by Random House Children's Books, 61-63 Uxbridge Road, London W5 5SA

www.kidsatrandomhouse.co.uk
www.randomhouse.co.uk

Addresses for companies within The Random House Group Limited can be found at: www.randomhouse.co.uk/offices.htm

THE RANDOM HOUSE GROUP Limited Reg. No. 954009

A CIP catalogue record for this book is available from the British Library.

Printed in China

In Africa, there was once a very, very mean lion.

One afternoon he gave Buffalo a wedgie,

he stuck a silly note on Zebra's back,

and he stole Hyena's lunch monkey.

Soon, all the animals were tired of his bullying.

But none of them was brave enough
to make Lion stop.

They needed help – so they asked Baboon to write
an advert and post it on the Internet.
This is what it said:

A Russian bear saw the advert and arrived in Africa on the next flight.

But although the bear was strong, he was no match for Lion.

Then a moose arrived from North America.

I'll make Lion stop!

But Lion was too quick for the moose.

Next came a tiger all
the way from India.

But, again, Lion won.
He was just too strong.

The bear, moose and tiger all caught
the next plane home.

It seemed that no one could stop Lion
from being so mean!

But just as Lion was about to carry on his bullying, one last animal arrived by boat.

WAIT!

It was a rabbit all the way from Europe.

"Because you're so small," said Lion,
"you can choose the contest."

"Alright, let's have a marshmallow-eating
competition," said Rabbit.

"That'll be easy," laughed Lion.

Lion ate three buckets of marshmallows before he started to feel sick.

But even though Rabbit was tiny,
he ate ten buckets!

"Not fair," said Lion,
"I wasn't feeling well."

"Alright then, let's have
a quiz," replied Rabbit.

Lion tried his best.

scratch
scratch

O

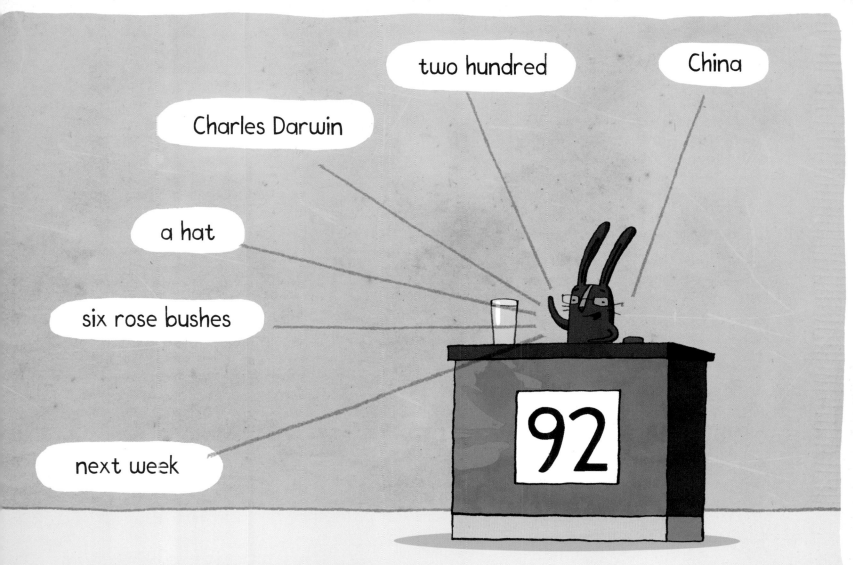

But Rabbit won the quiz by a hundred points.

"I wasn't ready," said Lion.

"Alright, let's have a hopping competition," replied Rabbit.

Lion started out really well, but he only
lasted ten minutes.

But Rabbit hopped non-stop for six hours!

"I wasn't warmed up," said Lion.

"Ok, let's have a painting competition," replied Rabbit.

Lion's picture was okay.

But Rabbit's picture
was much better.

"I was distracted,"
moaned Lion.

"Ok, we'll have one more
competition. You can
choose what it is."

Lion thought hard.

"Let's have a race to the top of the mountain. I'm faster, stronger and a better climber than you. There's no way I can lose!"

Lion was away even before the starting gun went off.

But after a few minutes,
Lion saw Rabbit up ahead of him.

Lion sprinted to catch up –
and overtook Rabbit.

But when he clambered up some rocks, he saw Rabbit ahead of him again.

Lion overtook Rabbit once more, and raced to the top of the mountain.

But as he got close . . .

. . . he saw that Rabbit was already at the top!

"You're an amazing rabbit,"
said Lion when he finally got there.
"You win, I'll stop bullying the animals."

That night all the animals gathered at
the harbour to give Rabbit his prize and
to wish him a safe journey home.

But to their surprise, there wasn't just one rabbit leaving on the boat . . .

There were ten rabbits full of marshmallows . . .

one brainy rabbit,

six hopping rabbits . . .

one arty rabbit . . .

and four cross-country rabbits.

Lion never did find out that the rabbits had tricked him –
who would want to tell him?
After all, the rabbits had just wanted to help and from that
day on Lion was never mean to anyone again.